For Trip —
You are THE BEST!
& Have the very best
Mom + Grandmom, too!
XO Debi & Iris

Iris
the Architect

Iris
the Architect

By
Debra Lampert-Rudman

FABULOUS BOOKS

www.fbs-publishing.co.uk

First Published in the UK August 2014 by FBS Publishing Ltd.

22 Dereham Road, Thetford, Norfolk. IP25 6ER

ISBN: 978-0-9560537-7-0

Illustrator and Text Copyright © Debra Lampert-Rudman 2014

A CIP catalogue record for this book is available from the British Library.

Cover Design and Illustrations by Debra Lampert-Rudman

Text Edited by Alasdair McKenzie

Typesetting by Scott Burditt

Paper stock used is natural, recyclable and made from wood grown in sustainable forests. The manufacturing processes conform to environmental regulations.

Dedication

*To the memory of my mother, Rose Lampert,
who always believed I was the best.*

Iris loved to draw.
She especially loved
drawing dog houses,
dog beds, and dog sleds.

Drawing made
her very happy.

"Iris, pencils down,"
Mama barked.
"We're late for
the dog show!"

Iris didn't like
dog shows.

They made her
very unhappy.

But every weekend
she went.

"Remember, dogs in *our* family are *champions*," Mama said, "the best of our breed."

On Saturday, Iris trotted home with a 2nd place ribbon.

"Next time you'll be first; you just need more practice," Mama yipped.

"*More practice*," Iris thought with a sly little smile. "*Yes, I definitely need more practice!*"

"Maybe I need more posing practice," Iris said.

"I'll be in the garage in front of the mirror every day before the next show."

But instead of posing,
Iris drew.
She drew dog houses,
dog doors,
and dog steps.

Iris was very happy.

On Saturday, Iris came home
with a 3rd place ribbon.

"Maybe I need more baths," Iris said.

"I'll take special spa bubble baths every day before the next show."

But, instead
of taking baths,
Iris drew in
the bathroom.

She drew
dog houses,
dog bowls,
and dog beds.

Iris was very happy.

That weekend, Iris came home
with a 4th place ribbon.

"Maybe I should eat more veggies,"
Iris said.

"I'll go out to the garden every day
before the next show, Mama."

Instead of eating veggies,
Iris drew in the garden.

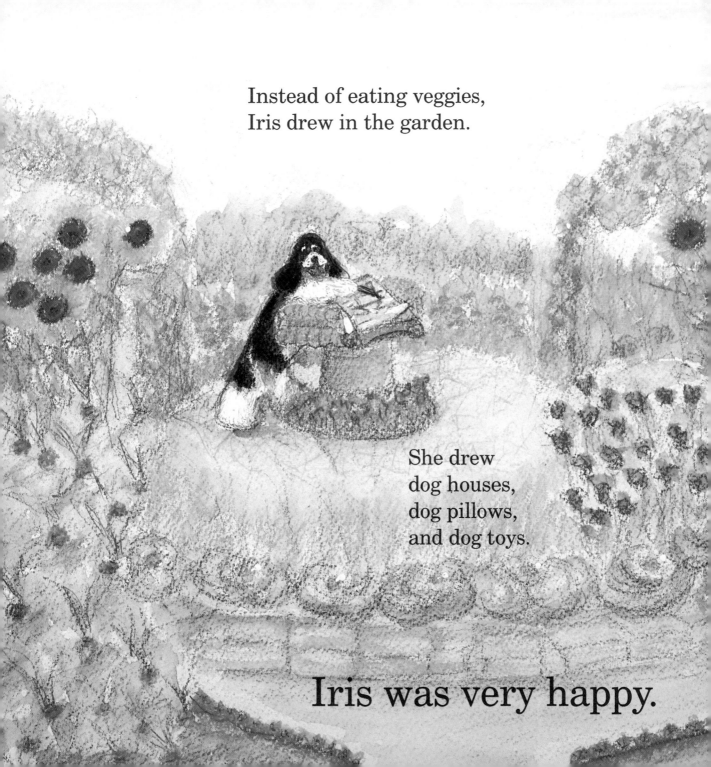

She drew
dog houses,
dog pillows,
and dog toys.

Iris was very happy.

That weekend, Iris didn't win a ribbon at all.

"I don't understand,"
Mama said, nuzzling Iris's ear.

"You take extra spa
bubble baths, practice posing,
and eat lots of vegetables.
You should win every time."

"I don't understand
it either," Iris said.

"I will try harder."

Off she ran to the garage to
"practice posing" some more.

While racing past the mirror,
Iris grabbed her pencils and said,
"Uh oh, looks like I'm out of paper.
Guess I'll draw on old newspapers."

The Spaniel Sentinel

Beagle

Suddenly,
Iris was *very*
happy.

The front page headline read:

Please Help Homeless Dogs!

"The Mayor is sponsoring a drawing contest to help homeless dogs. Winner's drawing to be built into a new home for homeless dogs. Entry deadline in six days."

Iris's next dog show was only six days away, too.

Iris ran into the house and yipped, "I want to win 1st place next week, Mama. I'm going to take spa bubble baths, practice posing, and eat tons of veggies every day for six days and

I'm going to win."

"That's the spirit, Iris," Mama howled. "You'll win the biggest, bluest ribbon ever!"

Iris drew every day,
for six days, and was very,
very happy.

*I know exactly what
homeless dogs
would love!*
Iris thought,
with a sly
little smile.

As she and Mama left for
Saturday's dog show ...

Iris ran to the
mailbox and
popped her contest
drawing inside.

That day,
Iris won

2nd place.

"You're getting there, Iris," Mama beamed. "See what practice can do."

Iris still didn't like dog shows. They still made her very unhappy.

But every weekend she went to dog shows with Mama, checking her mailbox on the way home.

"HOOOOOWWWWWWWWWWWWWWL"

"You have a letter from the Mayor, Iris!"
Mama howled.

"You have a letter from
the Mayor, Iris!"

"Iris, why do *you* have a letter from the Mayor?"

You and Your Family
Are
Cordially Invited
to the
Grand Opening
of our
New Home for Homeless Dogs
Designed by Iris

Saturday at 2:00 p.m.

R.S.V.P.

On Saturday,
Iris took a spa bubble bath,
ate some veggies and
posed in front of her
mirror in the garage …

Not for a dog show, but for a trip to City Hall.

The Mayor congratulated Iris.
Homeless dogs licked her and wagged their tails ...

Congratulations Iris!
Best Dog Architect!
Best Friend to Homeless Dogs!

Congratulations Iris!

Waving atop
The New Home
for Homeless Dogs,
designed by Iris, was
the biggest, bluest
ribbon Iris and
Mama had
ever seen.

"I always knew you were the best," Mama said, beaming.

Iris the Architect, Mama, and all their new friends smiled very big smiles and were very, very happy.

Author's Note

There really is an "Iris". Her "official" name is Ch. Topaz Purple Iris, CGC and she is a parti-color cocker spaniel who lives with me and four other champion cocker spaniels, including her great grandmother "Gigi", in Pennington, New Jersey, in the United States.

When she was a pup, Iris liked to jump on my husband Richard's lap and trying to grab his pencil and draw.

The real Iris enjoyed being a show dog and did become a champion, just like her mother, grandmother, great grandmother, and other show dogs in her family. Iris also does other fun things like going to obedience school, playing games like "Cocker Soccer" and is a Canine Good Citizen.

Iris is planning one more special thing: she may become a mom soon.
And, I'm sure she'll encourage her pups to be the best they can be, no matter what.

About the Author

Debra Lampert-Rudman grew up loving dogs, art, books, and writing and now lives in Pennington, New Jersey, US, where she is living her dream as a writer and artist, in the company of her dogs. Visit Debra, Iris and the rest of her dog family at www.potterypup.com

The illustrations in this book were done in watercolor pencil and acrylic

Discover more great books at www.fbs-publishing.co.uk

CPSIA information can be obtained at www.ICGtesting.com
Printed in the USA
BVIW12n2106261217
503743BV00011B/61